Copyright Matthew C

Edited by Matthew C.

All rights reserved. No part of this book may be reproduced in any form or by any means, except by inclusion of brief quotations in a review, without permission in writing from the publisher. Each author retains copyright of their own individual story.

This book is a work of fiction. The characters and situations in this book are imaginary. No resemblance is intended between these characters and any persons, living, dead, or undead.

This book is sold subject to the condition that it shall not, by way of trade or otherwise, be lent, resold, hired out or otherwise circulated without the publisher's prior consent in any form or binding or cover other than that in which it is published and without similar condition including this condition being imposed on the subsequent purchaser

Published in Great Britain in 2018 by Matthew Cash, Burdizzo Books Walsall, UK

THE CAT CAME BACK

MATTHEW CASH

Matthew Cash

The Very First Day

Darren Johnson thought his life was over. Well, that was how it felt anyway.

He smelled. He was scruffy, there was a hole in his left shoe to match the one in his heart, and he hadn't got a coat and the rain was coming down. He was a walking Blues song.

Every time he tried to light his fag the wind combined with the rain would extinguish the lighter's flame and threaten to dampen his cigarette beyond use. So, he took the slightly moist coffin-nail and ate it. The bitterness of the tobacco was quite moreish but he left it at just the one.

As he squelched back to his place, wind and hair plastering his face, he realised that he was not alone, even though when he turned around, he couldn't see anyone following.

It was that in-between time of night, too early for people to be going home, too late for people to be going to the pubs and clubs. No cars were on the road, apart from those parked along the roadside. Perhaps someone was spying on him from one of them. He carried on regardless but still, the sensation persisted.

Darren had a habit whenever he got this drunk, to rabbit along to himself, bitching about God knows who and fuck knows what. Alcohol amplified his inner monologue to the extent all of his thoughts were ranted and shouted out aloud like he was some filthy crab-infested tramp.

"Yeah, well I don't give a fucking shit, you stupid cunt. Fuck you, ugly fucking whore-bastard. Think I give a fuck what you do? Well, I don't. Fuck you," he shouted as he staggered up the road. Obviously, he did give a shit; otherwise, he wouldn't have been in this state for the fifth time in one week.

He wondered what day it was. Did he even care?

On the way up the steps to the tower block, he spotted G. He didn't know what his real name was. He couldn't pronounce it if he did. G was a big black man who reminded Darren of the chef out of that adult cartoon with the offensive school kids. He forever walked around in a big black puffer jacket like a Rastafarian Michelin man.

"All right, G, you great big, fat, black bastard?" Darren shouted at him. They had an understanding. He wasn't racist. He just said things as he saw them.

Two rows of teeth appeared in the night of his face like them tiny mint sweets.

"How you doing, Big Daddy?"

Darren hated it when he called him that. It reminded him of all those stupid fucking Father's Day T-shirts people buy. Number One Dad, Me? Nah, number one retard, more like. Any fucktard or inbred halfwit can become a father, it takes a lot more to become a Dad.

G told him that he had some work for the following day and to give him a bell around four, so he bumped shoulders with him and went to go inside.

There it was again, that weird sensation of being followed.

He spotted something out of the corner of his eye by the skips.

Turning as quickly as his intoxicated body would allow, he saw a ragged, scruffy grey cat staring at him.

He looked just as wet and fucked up as Darren felt.

"All right, cat?" he said as he opened the door to the block.

The cat peered pathetically up at him before sheepishly resting against his feet. He was drenched, the poor thing. He didn't know what came over him, a moment of charitable generosity or whatever, but he found himself letting the cat into the foyer.

Darren considered picking him up, but he looked so disgusting. Matted grey fur, dirty around his anus. One of his ears was half missing, due to some street fight, no doubt. He had read somewhere that cats were supposed to be clean animals. Obviously, Felix here hadn't read the same book. Realising that he wasn't exactly the cleanest of creatures either, he thought fuck it and scooped him up in his arms. He didn't resist at all, just stared with big, deep, yellow eyes.

"You smell like someone's pissed on you," Darren said to him as they got into the lift. He didn't think the cat understood but he answered with a puny, self-pitying meow. If a cat was capable of pouting sadly, then this cat was doing it.

By the time they had reached Darren's floor, he was purring alarmingly loud.

Once they got into the flat, Darren dropped him on the floor and told him to make himself at home. He walked up the hallway a few feet before stopping and meowing over his shoulder as if he was checking Darren was following. It was then that Darren had confirmation of his sex, massive cat bollocks. He stopped outside the kitchen door and spoke again.

How the fuck did he know that that was where the kitchen was? "I suppose you're fucking hungry?" He asked him and opened the kitchen door. He waltzed into the kitchen like he owned the place, sniffing all the crap on the floor, vacuuming up morsels of dropped food, crumbs, bits of fluff, God knew what.

Darren knew there wouldn't be anything in the cupboards for a cat to eat, about the only things he had in were baked beans. He stared at the tins before realising they were the type that had mini sausages in them.

If he was hungry, he'd eat them.

Darren got the lid off and spooned some of the beans into his mouth. A few blobs of sauce fell on his shirt and the floor. The cat flicked out his rough, little, pink tongue and cleaned it off the linoleum. "Quite handy, ain't you?"

Finding the first sausage, he dropped it to the floor for him. It was gone immediately. He never even paused to chew the damn thing.

Darren had another spoonful of beans and yelped as the cat sharpened his claws on his shin. "Oi, you bastard," he shouted, and the cat just stared up at him and meowed innocently.

"Fucking bastard," he growled at him and threw the three-quarters full tin of beans. The cat calmly dodged it and devoured the contents of the can within a few seconds. Not a drop was left on the floor, or his fur. He looked up at Darren, like Oliver Twist, asking for more.

"I ain't got no more, mate," Darren said and for some reason showed him his empty hands.

Darren was fucked and needed sleep drastically, so he ushered the cat out into the hallway. He grabbed an ashtray and filled it with water and stuck it on the floor. "That's for you to drink."

He meowed in response.

He laid a newspaper out on the floor near the front door. "That's for you to shit on and stuff."

Meow.

He switched the hall light off and went into his bedroom. He managed to get his top off and trousers around his feet before collapsing on the bed in a vegetative state.

Matthew Cash

The

Very

Next

Day...

The first thing he saw when he awoke was the pillowcase. The first thing he smelt was dry sweat and stale beer breath. Using every bit of energy he could muster, he rolled onto his side. His eyes took a while to focus on the cheap plastic digital alarm clock that faced him on the dusty, sticky bedside cabinet. The black digits took a while to transform from the black on grey blur, but, when it did, the first thing he noticed was that it said A.M.

A.M? *How was this possible?* Further inspection showed the digits at 5:34 A.M.

He couldn't remember the last time he had been awake at this time. It explained the dull grey glow of daylight coming through the thin curtains. He briefly wondered why he had woken so early. He cast an eye downward to make sure that he hadn't had an accident. The previous week he had that much to drink that he pissed the bed.

So, what had woken him up?

Flashes of the night before played in his head in black and white stills.

A bird's eye view of the first drink of the day, a pint of Guinness.

Beer garden for a fag.

Broken glass, angry barman.

Walking home in the rain.

Seeing G, the job offer.

Being followed, mangy cat.

Then it registered what had woken him up. At first, because he'd been hearing the noise every three seconds since he came to, it was so repetitive, he didn't notice it. But there it was.

And again.

And again.

And again, although that time slightly different, if possible, with a question mark at the end.

Meow.

Meow?

The cat.

Every three seconds, he could hear it speaking to him, followed by it trying to scratch its way under the door.

Half-bloody-five in the morning, for fuck sake. He grabbed the nearest thing to hand, a pillow, her pillow, and lobbed it at the door. Silence.

Meow?

Meow!

"Piss off," he yelled and hid his head beneath the pillow. He didn't need this. What he needed was another eight hours sleep, to get G's job done, and get back down to the pub. The furry bastard seemed to have stopped. He pulled the pillow aside.

Scratch, scratch, scratch. It was always three times, every time. Cat's got rhythm.

Meow.

Me-ow!

"That's it!" He jumped out of bed, too quick and too hungover. His head exploded, he collided with the wardrobe, tripped over his own trousers that were still around his ankles, and struck his head on the overflowing laundry basket.

"Fucking arsehole cat cunt."

To say Darren was livid would have been an understatement. He could see red. A giant red veil over his eyes obscured all rational sense of morality.

Darren always had a problem with his temper even though he was ashamed to admit it. It was one of the reasons she had left him.

He pulled open the bedroom door and was greeted by the space where the cat should have been. A streak of grey flashed past his feet and he heard the scritch-scratch of the feline's front claws on his expensive bed. He was about to haul its arse out of there when he saw the hallway.

To an unknown eye one might think he had been burgled. Half the contents of the bookcase were emptied all over the floor, shredded dust-jackets, long deep gouges in the wallpaper and the door frames. It wasn't until he walked up the hallway that he spotted several pools on the linoleum. Actually, it was slightly more than several. Ice-cold cat piss seeped into his socks. Humorously, to anyone but him, the newspaper he had lain down was spotless.

No shit, he thought he was lucky until he saw what lie on the front doormat.

The amount of shit that was heaped up on the floor was unnatural. There were shits of all shapes, sizes, and consistencies. A thick spray of diarrhoea was splattered up the door. A lump the size and shape of a cocktail sausage was welded to the wall. The smell was disgusting. His poor hungover stomach couldn't handle it. A jet of vomit took him by surprise, and he threw up on the pile of books on the floor. Tears welled up in his eyes. He couldn't take anymore. He needed sleep.

Darren turned to go back into the bedroom with the intention of sticking the cat back in the hallway. He could hardly do any more damage. He planned to get rid of him later.

Darren went back into the bedroom, and there it was. Slightly crouched, head jutting back and forth as a long, lumpy, furry torrent of silver cat spew erupted from its dirty mouth and on to his pillow. There was, what appeared to be, a mouse tail in it.

"Fucking dirty bastard!" Darren shrieked wiping the back of his hand across his mouth to stem the flow of more vomit. The cat arched its back and hissed at him.

"Cunt," he cursed as one of the cat's paws slashed at his reaching hand. Five perfect dotted red lines filled with blood. Darren seized the cat by its scruff and lifted it off his bed. It bucked and twisted itself in his grip, back legs pedalling away eager to gouge his forearms.

Darren opened his front door, smearing a semi-circle streak of thick cat shit over the floor, and threw the cat onto the landing. It swore as it bounced off the lift door and landed in a defensive crouch.

"Fuck you," Darren said, slamming the front door.

He spun around angrily and his bare feet instantly slid on the shit smear. Darren fell heavily on his arse. His feet and back were dirty with cat excrement. His left hand and elbow splashed in a lake of cat urine, and his head struck the floor, cushioned by the heap of vomit he had made. He wondered how his life could get any worse.

Meow. Scratch, scratch, scratch.

Fucking cat.

Darren groaned, ignored the noise outside his front door and set about cleaning the place, and himself, up.

It had taken nearly two hours to tidy all the mess the cat had made, and for the entire duration of that, he could hear the bloody thing asking to get back in. It was truly driving him insane. Not wanting to open the door to the fucking feline but having to do something to stop the bloody racket, Darren reluctantly pulled his coat on and opened the door. Instinctively, he stuck a foot around the door and pushed the grey bastard away as it tried to snake its way in. "Out. Fuck off."

The cat hissed at him and swiped at his shoe.

Darren locked the door behind him and called the lift. "What you going to do now? Come, follow me outside. We'll play in the road."

Meow.

The cat rubbed itself around his feet as soon as it had heard the change in Darren's tone.

The lift pinged and Darren stepped in, holding an arm out to stop the door from closing. "Come on, fuckface," he said softly with a smile on his face rubbing his thumb against his forefingers.

The cat yawned, as if bored, cast one look at the closed front door and padded into the lift.

Darren made sure the cat followed him outside of the building, and, as soon as they were both outside, he ran. The cat watched him half-interested as he fled for the next tower block.

Darren buzzed up, and someone answered the intercom amongst a cacophony of reggae music.

G's place reeked of marijuana. Darren stood in the centre of his living room, staring at the hardcore pornography on the plasma TV screen. He never really understood why people watched pornography for other reasons than masturbation purposes. What else was it for?

A heavily made up, ebony-skinned woman milked two scarily big, black erections onto her two equally scary gigantic bulging, black breasts. G shoved a jiffy envelope into his hand. "Now go, boy. I got shit to sort." G shoved a warm folded twenty-pound note into Darren's other hand.

Hoping and praying that the money wasn't warm from G's cock, Darren left G's place to make his delivery.

Well, that was a piece of piss, Darren thought, whistling happily whilst he walked away from the drop off's house. Easy money. He didn't dwell on what had been in the package G had him deliver. It didn't take much to guess, and he wasn't going to ask any questions.

Running errands delivery around the place for G kept him in money until he would get his benefits again. Hopefully, G would have another for him later or the next day, and, at twenty quid a time, he wouldn't refuse.

Darren flipped his vibrating mobile phone from out of his coat pocket and held it to his ear without checking the caller. "Hello?"

"Hey, Daz, where are you?" A woman's voice asked.

Shit, it's Fiona. "All right?" he answered blankly, not wanting to sound any emotion in his voice. He didn't want her to know he missed her like mad and was still devastated by her leaving.

"Where are you? I hope you ain't doing shit for that black bastard."

"Nah, nah, I was out having a run." Darren lied and cursed himself for lying. Another reason why she had left.

"Running? Drug running more like."

Darren's anger started to flare. He didn't have to answer to her anymore, she'd left him. "Look, you got something to say, say it or else I'm hanging up."

"I thought we should meet up, talk about things, have something to eat."

His face lit up as he failed to hide getting his hopes up. "Yeah? Day after tomorrow, I'll cook."

Fiona seemed impressed by Darren's suggestion and eagerly agreed to meet up with him.

Darren smiled and there was a spring in his step as he jogged back to his flat. Things may finally be looking up, he considered, forgetting all about the cat.

Matthew Cash

The

Very

Next

Day...

Darren pushed his sunglasses up the bridge of his nose and opened his front door. He looked down at his doormat. "For fuck sake."

The cat was curled up in a big ball on the threadbare mat. It flexed its claws and stretched its mouth wide open in a yawn. Its teeth stood out long and white against its mouth's black interior. As it yawned, a strangely elongated meow accompanied it. Opening one lazy eye, it unfurled from its cosy position and greeted Darren.

Darren slammed the front door closed before the wretched thing got into his flat and pressed the button on the lift. When the lift opened, he bent down and picked it up. The cat's protest was evident by the doormat that came along with it; attached to four sets of claws.

There was nothing else for it, thought Darren. I'm going to have to go see Cat-Man.

The lift stopped halfway down, and the door slid open onto a communal landing. The door to the flat opposite stood ajar, and a big fat ginger cat lay on the doorstep. It took one look at Darren and the grey cat before hissing and vanishing within the flat. Darren knocked on the door, "Stan?"

Stan, Cat-Man to the majority of people in the flats, appeared in the doorway. He was a small, old, but spritely, man, with a huge white beard. He eyed the grey cat in Darren's arms and smiled. "Oh hello, and who's this?"

Darren smiled, "He hasn't got a name," Well none that I can call him in front of you. "He's a stray, followed me home the other night. If it wasn't for my girlfriend being allergic, I'd keep him, honestly."

Cat-Man Stan looked sympathetic. "Well, there's always room for another moggy. Come in."

Darren followed Stan into his flat.

It was the same layout as his but far more cluttered. A whole forest of assorted cat scratching posts ran along one wall.

A four-foot square area was taken up by four litter trays. Cats of all shapes and colours waltzed in and out of the different rooms; the doors were all left open. Darren counted at least eight different felines. Surprisingly, the place appeared and smelled clean despite its many inhabitants.

Darren walked up the hallway cradling what he hoped would be Cat-Man's latest addition. All the cats that spotted them fled into the furthest room.

"So, how many do you have?" Darren asked.

Cat-Man Stan scratched his beard and thought for a moment. "I have fourteen living with me, and there must be at least a dozen who I leave food out for outside; waifs, strays, ones that want a bit extra to eat."

"Blimey," Darren said smiling, confident that he had brought the pesky pussy to the right place. "You'll be happy here." He said, faking his best caring voice for the animal he had fast learned to despise.

The cat went stiff as a board, still clinging to the doormat, as Darren handed him, doormat and all, to Cat-Man Stan. The old man chuckled as he accepted his latest flatmate. "Don't worry, he'll settle in once he's got his bearings and met all the others."

He attempted but failed, to pry the doormat from the cat's claws. "I'll drop this off later."

Darren thanked him for accepting his burden and left the flat with a spring in his step.

Darren spent the rest of the day chilling out with a few beers on the balcony. The sun was blazing and he felt amazing. He had finally got the pesky vermin in somewhere with someone who wanted him. He had images of the cat making friends with Cat-Man's herd. Was herd the right word for a collected group of cats? He didn't think it sounded right, maybe a pack? Nah, that was dogs. A posse of pussies. Darren snorted into his beer,

"Pussy Posse. Sounds like a fucking porno."

He thought about the mess the cat had made of his flat in just one night. Maybe a cunt of cats was more appropriate.

The...

Very...

Next...

Day...

Darren yawned and stretched. He kicked his boxer shorts towards the laundry basket in the corner of the bedroom and opened the door. A shot of grey whizzed past his feet. "What the fuck?" he shouted; spinning round in the direction it went in.

There.

On his bed.

The cat. The cat.

It sat in a patch of sunshine on his duvet, legs tucked beneath its body; its tail jutted out across the bed, the tip twitching like a rattlesnake. Its yellow eyes looked at him once before closing.

Darren was astonished. *How the fuck did he get back in?*

The first thing he did was check his front door. All four locks were still fastened.

The letterbox?

Darren mentally compared the size of the letterbox and the cat.

No way.

His mind brought back an episode of The X Files, where one of their best baddies, a guy called Tooms had the ability to stretch himself as though he were made of rubber like one of those stress relief toys.

He had images of the cat squeezing itself through the letterbox, similar to the bad guy in The X Files.

Darren picked up some clothes from the laundry basket and unlocked his front door. His doormat was back, so obviously, Cat-Man Stan had been up here at some point. Maybe he was a master lock-picker, and had gotten pissed off with the cat, and wanted to return it but couldn't rouse him? It was the only thing he could think of, even though it did seem a trifle far-fetched.

Darren slowly approached the bed. The cat stared as he reached out to pick it up.

A low rumble like distant thunder came from its throat, and it swiped a claw at him, lightning quick.

Darren recoiled just in the nick of time, and, whilst the cat was distracted by his one hand, he grabbed it by the scruff with the other.

It twisted and pivoted and tried its best to bite him or claw whatever it could reach, but Darren had started to get wise to the wily bastard. Holding it at arm's length, he marched out of his flat and called the lift.

Cat-Man Stan's face went white when he saw Darren at the door.

Probably thinks I'm going to nut him or something, Darren considered.

Cat-Man just stood staring at the cat, shaking his head.

"So, what's up?" Darren said, pushing the cat towards the old man.

"You'd better come in," Cat-Man said mournfully.

Darren entered the man's flat and noticed the difference straight away. Criss-crosses of scratches lined almost every door in the hallway, and the linoleum was equally shredded.

The place smelt strongly of bleach and he noticed that all the cat-related paraphernalia was gone.

Cat-Man led Darren through to his kitchen after telling him to leave the cat in the hallway.

Darren didn't really want to stop and chat but could tell that there was something up with the old guy, and, if he expected him to take the problem feline back, the least he could do was hear him out.

"It was horrible," Cat-Man Stan said. His old rheumy eyes staring into his Garfield mug, "I went out for a pint, as I sometimes do, and left all the cats in the hallway like normal, so they could have food, drink and do their business. I left Bailey..." He paused and nodded towards the closed kitchen door, "That's what I called him. I left Bailey in the kitchen seeing as it was his first night, I didn't want the others ganging up on him, because they weren't used to him. But, somehow, maybe I had left a window open, as sometimes the draught can open the doors, he got into the hallway."

Darren stole a glance through the glass hatch between the kitchen and living room. He couldn't see a cat anywhere. He started feeling cold about what Cat-Man was going to tell him.

Cat-Man Stan wiped his eyes on his maroon cardigan sleeve, "When I came back, by God, it was a ruddy bloodbath."

"Shit, what happened?" Darren said, even though he thought he knew the answer.

"When I was a lad, I grew up on my father's farm, and he always had a few cats about. They kept rodent infestation down and were relatively cheap pets. I always played with them, they were my friends. The boss of the bunch was a great big scruffy ginger tom who I called Big Jim." Cat-Man smiled at his reminiscence.

"Big Jim was a monster, a rough male who made sure all the others knew who was in charge. He'd have his pick of the females and would usually be first at the food bowl, even though he rarely ate cat food. He preferred to catch and kill stuff you see, like a wild cat."

Cat-Man sipped at his drink and wiped the droplets from his white moustache.

"Well, one summer, we had a big problem with rats, big bastards they were, too. My father wouldn't lay poison as, well, that's what the cats were for.

We found the nest near the old barn, and Dad took Big Jim and a couple of the other cats over to it.

Dad shoved a stick down the hole, and all Hell broke loose.

Four dirty, great big black rats bolted out of the nest, I've never seen ones as big before, or since. Big Jim pounced on one, and I saw him rip its throat out. I actually saw him tear its throat out within a second of seeing it! He jumped on another and did the same. It was ferocious. He was vicious. Dad saw one rat off with his spade, chopped the poor blighter right in half, he did. I swear its front half ran for two feet before it realised it had left its arse and back legs behind. The other rat got away. The other cats actually ran away from it."

"What happened here, Stan?" Darren said, trying not to sound impatient but actually wanting to be gone before the old man started crying properly.

Cat-Man raised his mug to his lips with a trembling hand, "He had killed them all."

Darren screwed his face up in disbelief. "What the fuck? How the hell could one cat take on fourteen?" He could see Cat-Man Stan was telling the truth but still needed an explanation.

Cat-Man shook his head, "I don't know. But he did. When I came home the lino was awash with blood.

The place smelled of cat piss and blood. They were everywhere. I had to pick claws that had been torn out from the doors and flooring. Obviously, the others had put up a fight. Who wouldn't if they were trapped in somewhere with a demon? But they lay strewn about the place like bloodied rags. Chunks of fur with skin attached, bits of God know what everywhere. And that thing," Cat-Man pointed a bony finger at the kitchen door, "that abomination, it sat there, covered in red, washing itself as if it hadn't a care in the world."

"What did you do?" Darren asked. He still wanted to know how the cat, Bailey, as he had been christened by Cat-Man Stan, managed to get outside his bedroom door.

Cat-Man was unable to control his tears, he wept openly. "You must understand, I would never hurt an animal, especially a cat, but after what he had done…."

Darren reached forward and patted Cat-Man's shoulder. "It's all right, I understand that, of course, I do. But what did you do?"

Cat-Man sniffed back snot, and his hurt turned to anger, as he stared through the closed kitchen door and back to the previous night's massacre. "I kicked the fucking thing's cunt in!"

Darren's eyes went wide at Cat-Man Stan's coarse language. It didn't suit the sweet, little, old man exterior. He needn't worry too much, though, as his anger extinguished as quickly as it ignited; and he broke down in tears again. "I kicked him and kicked him until he was just as ragged and ruined as the rest of them. It was an evil, barbaric thing to do, I know that. I stuck him in the bag with the rest of them."

Darren stared at his own teacup as he tried to register Cat-Man's words.

He couldn't have hurt it like he thought. Either that or it was a different cat.

"Are you sure you, err... killed him?"

Cat-Man nodded, "I felt his skull crush beneath my shoe. That is not a normal cat."

Darren shook his head in disbelief. The old man must be senile or winding him up something stupid. He slammed his cup down hard on the table and stood up. "This is bullshit. I'm going, I'll get rid of the stupid animal myself, ring RSPCA or something."

Darren stormed out of the kitchen, pushed Bailey, who stood right behind the door, as though listening, in the direction of the front door and shouted, "Out."

The cat meowed at him and followed him out of Cat-Man's flat.

"Fucking senile old twat," Darren muttered as he waited for the lift.

He had to bloody wait four hours for the RSPCA to send somebody out to get the cat. Four hours, and then the bloody thing went insane, and it took both Darren and the RSPCA man to get it in the cage.

When Darren had told him his predicament, not mentioning giving it to the cat enthusiast a few floors below, the RSPCA man nodded smugly and said it was a regular occurrence. The cat was obviously a stray, a streetwise animal.

He would be slowly becoming feral, on his guard against potential threats and competition. Was no doubt used to fighting for everything. The worst thing Darren had done, according to the man, was keep him confined in his flat. It had obviously made the cat distraught. It wasn't surprising that he had wrecked the place.

Still trying to fathom out how the bloody thing got into his flat, Darren breathed a sigh of relief when the RSPCA man drove off in his little, white van.

Darren checked his watch and tutted. Fiona was always late. He should have been used to it, but with how eager she had sounded on the phone, and with the several text messages she had sent supplementing that, he thought she would be on time. He dished out the Chinese take away onto two plates and stuck them in the oven on a low heat to keep warm. The front door buzzer went. "Shit!" He ran up the hallway and picked up the white handset. "Hello?"

"Hello," called the excited Fiona, "let me in, let me in."

"All right, babe." Darren pressed Enter and hung up the receiver. Back to the kitchen to discreetly hide any evidence that he hadn't just purchased the lovingly prepared, homemade Chinese cuisine, Fiona's favourite.

Fiona jumped towards him and pressed her mouth hard against his, her arms hugging him so tight he thought his ribs would crack.

"I've missed you so fucking much," she said when she finally broke away. He smiled sheepishly and let her into the flat. He checked her out as she walked through the hall towards the kitchen, admiring her figure-hugging black dress. Even though it had only been a fortnight since he had seen her last, when they had had the fight and split up, she looked as though she had lost weight or toned up.

"Man, you're looking fit as fuck!" Darren said without thinking and mentally cursed himself for being so blatant. But it didn't seem to bother Fiona, who laughed coyly over her shoulder before sitting down at the table.

"Right, I've made your favourite, king prawn curry, just like they do at the Chinese place," Darren said, opening the oven. "I got a recipe off the internet and everything."

He bent down to reach for the plates when Fiona's black stilettoed foot kicked the door shut. Darren gulped, and his eyes rode up her black stockings, and eventually, they found their way up to her face.

"If you don't bend me over this table right now, Darren Johnson, I'll shove that take away Chinese so far up your arse you'll spit rice for a week!"

Fuck, thought Darren, as he fumbled as quickly as he could with his belt buckle and trousers, this was one pussy he was glad to see back.

Darren sighed and put his arm around Fiona's bare shoulders. The feel of her next to him again was sublime, like he had been reunited with a missing jigsaw piece. He felt completed. She nuzzled into his neck and kissed him as they lay in the bed. He didn't even mind that her long dark hair was all over his face. It used to annoy him, but now he welcomed it.

"Sorry I was late, Daz. There was a massive pile up on the motorway," Fiona said, tracing a finger across his chest.

"Don't worry about it," he said, kissing her on top of her head. "Bloody rush hour, weren't it? It's to be expected."

Fiona sat up on one elbow. "You know what the worst thing about it was?"

Darren shook his head.

"Some poor bastard was killed outright. His van had a head-on with a fucking Eddie Stobart lorry."

"Jesus! Who was on the wrong side of the bloody road?" Darren said. He wasn't overly concerned for people he didn't know but thought his reaction was showing that he was capable of sincerity.

"The van driver," Fiona replied.

"Typical! Bloody white van drivers are all the fucking same. Stupid idiot could have driven into a school bus or something." Good touch with the school bus, he congratulated himself.

"That's not the worst of it," Fiona said wide-eyed.

"Oh?"

"There were loads of animals killed."

"What the fuck? Was it a horsebox or something?"

"No, an RSPCA van. Those poor little animals, being rescued and then…."

"Fuuuuuuuuck!" Darren screamed and leapt from the bed, scaring the life out of Fiona. He ran bare-arsed into the hallway and opened a cupboard door, which he kept tools and stuff in. Fiona watched completely dumbfounded as Darren frantically used almost a whole reel of duct tape to seal the letterbox.

Darren slumped down on the bed and breathed with relief.

"What was that all about?" Fiona said sitting up.

Darren peered over his shoulder at her, not wanting to tell her the unrealistic truth, he chose to lie. "Fucking kids put a firework through the letterbox the other day."

Fiona frowned. "So how did you get from my road crash incident to a firework?"

Shit! He cursed inwardly. "I think it was because you mentioned a school bus."

"You mentioned the school bus," she corrected him and patted the bed beside her. "Were you all right? The stupid idiot could have started a fire. You should report it."

Darren lay down beside her and shook his head. "Nah, I was fine. They were just kids pissing about. I was the same."

"If it happens again, you're reporting it, okay?" Fiona said with disapproval. "Promise."

Darren smiled reassuringly and nodded. "I will. I promise."

Fiona whipped back the duvet, unveiling her nudity. "Now, come over here stick your firework through my letterbox."

"Oh, that's bad," Darren said, groaning and laughing at Fiona's bad joke, but he did as instructed.

Darren watched as the RSPCA man crawled across the tarmac from the van's wreckage. His left leg had been crushed in the collision, and he dragged it behind him as he desperately tried to flee the burning vehicle. A stereotypical, yellow, American school bus lay on its side. Children spilled from the windows like burst innards.

Darren tried to shout at them to hurry before something exploded, but his mouth didn't seem to be working. A weight was on his chest, and his throat felt obstructed.

All he could hear was the long drag of the RSPCA man's ruined leg, like a fingernail being slowly scratched across sandpaper.

The lump in his throat moved upwards, and he retched, his head darting back and forth like an excited chicken. He opened his mouth and gagged as an egg-sized, grey lump flew out on a geyser of pink sick.

Darren stared as the grey lump pulsated and expanded and unfolded itself into the cat, or Bailey, as he had been christened by Cat-Man. It stretched and pounced onto the RSPCA man. With an unbelievable amount of strength, it bit into the man's undamaged leg and started to drag him back to the vehicle. His terrified face pleaded for help. Nothing but wet gurgling gasps came when he spoke.

Darren began to wake up, the gasps of the RSPCA man continued with the transition from sleep to awake, but he didn't open his eyes.

Darren knew what the gasping was. The weight he had felt on his chest had moved down to his abdomen, but he was more focused on another sensation.

Fiona was licking his cock. His foggy head didn't question the roughness of her tongue, just accepted the gasping as she was obviously enjoying herself in the throes of passion. He wondered if she was touching herself while she pleasured him. He had trouble willing himself awake so he could properly join in the fun until his cock twitched and intense pain pierced the shaft.

Darren opened his eyes and screamed. The first thing he saw was the little puckered circle of skin that was a cat's arsehole. Four sets of claws dug into his belly and thighs, as the cat bit down on his penis.

Darren grabbed at the animal around its hind legs, but this just infuriated it more. He turned to call for help. That was when he saw the source of the gasping noise. Fiona was sat up in the bed, face purple, fingers clawing at her throat, as she fought for breath.

Her allergy! Darren, and jumped off the bed despite the cat still being attached. The pain was phenomenal, excruciating.

He moved across the bedroom in some weird insane dance, swearing and beating his fists at the grey stripy vermin as it clung to him.

Darren thrust himself, crotch first, at the bedroom door, pushing the door open and dislodging the cat. Before it could get away, he grabbed it by the scruff and hurled it into the bathroom opposite. The cat shrieked as it collided with the cheap medicine cabinet and knocked it off the wall. Darren quickly closed the door and ran to get the telephone.

As he dialled treble nine, he saw Fiona's eyes bulging as she struggled to get oxygen.

He looked down at the blood pouring from his penis, and one thing crossed his mind…

The

Cat

Had

Come

Back.

Darren sat in the waiting room at the hospital, absentmindedly watching the muted television on the wall.

What the fuck is the point of having the television on if it's on mute?

Was it just for something to do?

Do hospitals have excess electricity to burn? Why hadn't they stuck the subtitles on like they do when they stick it on in the pub? He thought it was daft.

He checked the clock on the wall. He had sat in the waiting room for nearly two hours. When he had arrived at the hospital with Fiona in the ambulance, they had told him he wasn't allowed to go in with her. He had to go to the reception and give her details and get someone to check out his injuries. Funnily enough, he had only had to wait five minutes to be seen for his cat scratches and bites. When the nurse had cleaned away all the blood, it didn't look half as bad as it felt. He was sent away with a tube of antiseptic cream and was waiting for news on Fiona.

The end credits of whatever was on the television started rolling, and a nurse walked into the waiting room. "Are you Darren?"

Darren stood.

He detected a sympathetic expression on her face. *Oh shit,* he thought, *it's bad news.*

He put his hands over his face, preparing himself for the worst. Visions flashed past his eyes, of him getting down on one knee and doing the honourable thing, him getting a job to support Fiona and their future children. Them growing old together, maybe going on a canal boat holiday on the Norfolk Broads; whatever they were.

The nurse smiled sympathetically and started speaking, "I'm afraid I have some bad news."

"Oh, Christ, no," Darren sobbed, tears in his eyes, "I was going to propose to her. I know we had been fighting, but I would forgive her anything."

The nurse pushed her palms up. "Whoa, slow down. She's fine."

Darren breathed a sigh of relief and laughed joyously, "Oh, thank God." He wiped at his eyes, "Sorry for all that. I just love her."

The nurse's facial expression still hadn't changed. Darren thought she should really try to be more self-aware of her facial expressions.

"She was fine after about half an hour of getting here. She asked me to give you this." The nurse shoved a folded piece of paper into his hand and hastily sped away.

Darren opened the note and saw the familiar scruffy handwriting he only ever saw in greeting cards.

Daz,

A cat? A fucking cat? You've proved how quickly you've gotten over me. Got yourself a new pet as soon as I went, did you? One that you know I'm highly allergic to, you cunt. Keep the fucking animal because you haven't got me. I came back to give us another go, to see if you were better than the other man that's shown me interest. But you've shown me what you're like.

Fuck you and your stinking cat. I hope it smothers you in your sleep.

Fiona

Darren collapsed onto the chair and reread the note. How could she think he had gotten the cat as a vindictive reaction to her walking out on him? It was absurd. Wouldn't another woman make more sense, not a fucking cat? He felt like running to her, explaining to her what had been happening, this cat that wouldn't leave him the fuck alone. Cat-Man Stan would back him up, surely? But then he reread the note again, hoping that he had misread the part about another man; he hadn't.

Another man.

Just the fact that there was another man, a rival, was enough for him to admit defeat.

Fuck her.

He screwed the note into a ball and flicked it at the television.

The fucking cat had done him a favour.

For a split second, he debated keeping the thing, but the needle pricks in his cock changed his mind.

The further he got from the hospital, the more the anger boiled inside of him.

Darren ignored the sound of hisses, feline swearing and claws on wood, and pulled a heavy duty backpack out of a cupboard. He shut all of the doors in the hallway and zipped up his denim jacket. He pulled on thick thermal gloves and reached for the bathroom door handle. He was taking no more chances with the fucking cat. Beneath the denim jacket he wore two T-shirts and a leather jacket. He had two pairs of pants and jeans on, too.

He pulled open the door an inch, and a long grey foreleg shot through the gap, claws out and splayed, like Krueger's glove.

Darren pushed the door open, hard, and took great satisfaction when it slammed into the cat. The moment the door was open the cat jumped towards Darren's face, the only part of him uncovered.

A quick searing burn rose on his cheek as the cat collided with him. Darren grabbed it around the belly and held it at arm's length as it twisted and tried to free itself. It appeared to be demonic, ears flat against its head, lips drew back as it bared its teeth.

Darren lowered the writhing beast towards the backpack, but its legs were everywhere, preventing him from getting it in.

All the trouble this wretched cat had caused made Darren flip his lid, and somehow, in a fit of rage, he managed to get the fucking, bucking feline in the bag.

Darren fastened the drawstring and clasps and leant back against the radiator to catch his breath. The bag shifted about as the cat tried to escape. Tiny needlepoint claws poked through the bag's thick material.

Let's get this over with, Darren thought. He bent down, scooped up the rucksack, and left to go to G's.

G took one last toke on the spliff before dropping the butt in the empty beer can. He had listened to Darren's tale about this badass cat with a straight face. "So, what you're basically saying is this cat is one nasty bitch and won't leave you alone?"

Darren nodded stupidly, the rucksack shaking like mad in his hands. "Just take it as far away as possible and dump it in a river. I don't care what you do with it, actually, just as long as it doesn't come back."

G scratched his black, fuzzy beard. "And you say this boy took on and killed fourteen others, all at once?"

Darren didn't like the look on G's face. He was plotting something. "Yeah, man, fourteen. Look, man, this fucking thing is dangerous, indestructible."

G grinned widely as he took the bucking rucksack out of Darren's hands and brought it close to his face. "Meow!" he said close to the material and flinched when two sets of claws poked through, mere centimetres from his face. G chuckled loudly and winked mischievously at Darren. "I'll do a deal with you, Big Daddy, you, me and Felix, here, go for a little ride now, and, afterwards, I'll maybe dump the kitty for free. You cool?"

Darren nodded slowly, he knew better than to refuse one of G's offers. "Okay, for fuck sake, man."

The warehouse looked derelict from the outside, but G knew better. He rapped a gold-ringed knuckle against the rusted metal door. After a few seconds, a scrawny little man slid the door back. He smiled at G and eyed Darren suspiciously. "All right, G-Man, what's happening?" the little man said, standing in the doorway as he and G bumped fists.

"Tay, me and my boy, Daz, here, wanna come in."

Tay, the little man, grinned widely, showing filthy discoloured teeth. "Great, great, come on in, lads. So, you pair wanting a little flutter this afternoon?" He slammed the door closed and drew a bolt across before leading them further into the building.

Darren wondered what the hell he was being led into. The building was empty aside from a few leftover pieces of rubbish from squatters or vandals. G's friend was leading them towards a door at the back of the large area they were in.

"Nah, man, we're wanting to participate. We have ourselves a fighter," G said and chuckled at Tay's confused expression.

"You mean your mate?" Tay said, nodding towards Darren worriedly.

"No. No way. I'm not fighting anyone," Darren said nervously, looking to G for confirmation.

G roared with laughter. "No," he pointed to the rucksack Darren carried, "our fighter's in there, boss."

Tay grinned. "Well, unless it's a fucking chihuahua with a tendency to turn into the incredible fucking hulk when it's angry, it's going to get ripped apart. Some right nasty bastards here today, I can tell you." Tay took out a key and unlocked a door they had stopped in front of. When he opened it, from within the next room came the noise of dozens of excited individuals.

A crowd of mostly men gathered around a circular ring constructed of wooden pallets lashed together with ropes. Darren past a few people who held leads with nasty vicious looking dogs straining against the chains. The dogs looked just as full of anger, hatred, and testosterone as their equally vicious owners. Animalistic grunting and snarls came from the ring, which spurred the crowd to cheer. Money changed hands. A few men seemed livid. Darren had a bad feeling about this.

The man G called Tay pushed through the throng to get to the ringside. A few words were shouted that were indecipherable before Darren caught the sentence, "We have a winner!"

A fat man in a tracksuit smiled triumphantly, and two other men moved one of the pallets as he bent down and fastened a collar and lead to the victorious winner. The crowd parted to key the dog and its happy owner through. Darren felt sickened as the fat man pushed past him. The dog, a thick muscular white bull terrier, panted and limped behind him. Its white fur was pink and crisscrossed with abrasions. A black patch covered one of its eyes like Bill Sykes' Bullseye, the eye swollen bloody and closed. Its jaws hung open. Slivers of red meat dangled from between its teeth. Its breathing sounded ragged and laboured.

G clamped hands with the fat man in the tracksuit. "Congratulations, man, you make it to the semis?"

The fat man nodded ecstatically. "Yeah, you bet yah. Gotta go clean the fucker up now. He's only got a fortnight to recuperate."

G patted him on the shoulder and went to speak to Tay.

Darren was at a loss of what to do. He had finally realised what G was intending to do in this warehouse that reeked of marijuana, body odour, and dog excrement. Even though he wanted to be rid of the cat, he thought this was unnecessary. He didn't give a shit how the cat was gotten rid of, but this was just brutal.

He decided that he would try and dump the cat himself.

Pushing his way through the people to catch up with G, he tapped one of his big bear-like shoulders. G span around and showed him a mouthful of teeth. "Here he is, my main man, Daz."

Before Darren had a chance to utter a syllable, G yanked the rucksack out of his hands and gave it to Tay, who called for silence.

"Now," the little man shouted, "we've got a new contender." He raised the bag in the air to a chorus of laughter. "Who wants to take it on?"

A few hands went in the air, owners offering their dogs up for the challenge, even though they didn't know what was in the rucksack. Why would they care? It wasn't like they themselves would get hurt.

Darren tried to get G's attention but was pushed aside as the crowd closed in on the ring to get a look at what was going on.

He heard Tay shout. "We have an opponent, stick it in the ring."

He pushed his way through the men and leant against the wooden pallets for a better view, and to try and locate G.

A huge black dog was let into the ring. Darren wasn't sure on the breed, but he thought it looked like one of the ones that had been recently banned, a Pitbull. It padded into the ring on long thick legs. It paid no attention to the cheering crowd other than its owner, a middle-aged skinhead covered with facial tattoos.

Darren spotted G, caught his eye and shook his head vigorously, but G just laughed, loosened the drawstrings and fasteners on the rucksack, and dropped it into the ring.

Everyone waited in silent anticipation for what surprise lurked inside the rucksack. There had even been side bets on what it contained; the favourite was some kind of wild animal, a badger, or maybe a ferret-- something that had to be vicious for G to suddenly enter the competition. All eyes were on the black opening to the bag.

A few laughs of disbelief and disappointment surfaced when the crowd witnessed a scruffy, grey tabby cat strut out of the bag and stop a few feet away from it. The cat ignored the people and cocked a leg behind its head and proceeded to lick its arse and balls.

The room was silent as they waited for something to happen. The black dog's owner shouted something to the animal, and the dog walked slowly across the ring. A low threatening growl rumbled deep within its throat. The cat paused mid-lick and spotted the dog approaching and changed its position. It arched its back, stretched out its front legs, and yawned.

The skinhead dog owner shouted out another command and the dog bared its teeth and launched itself at the cat. Within a heartbeat, the dog had the cat around the belly in its powerful jaws and was shaking it like a dirty rag. The cat hissed and spat and struck out its front claws in one swipe that made the dog yelp and drop it instantly. The cat backed off, its fur down its spine and tail rigid with fright. The feline and canine circled each other, both animals riled up by an opponent that was tougher than they expected.

The dog was used to fighting other dogs. It didn't like the cat's dexterity and flexibility, and the needle-like claws that had done something to make its eyes blurry.

The cat was used to fighting off anything and everything but wasn't used to being attacked so instantly and dramatically, and it wasn't used to its opponents coming back for more. One swipe at a dog usually sent them packing.

The people watching the match went wild, and more cash was bet on the outcome of what looked like it could be an epic fight.

The skinhead man shouted commands angrily. There was no way he was letting a fucking cat get the better of his prizefighter. He reached across into the ring and screamed at his dog.

The dog reluctantly went in for another attack, but the cat was ready. It darted between the dog's front legs, twisted around onto its back, and attached itself to the dog's pendulous testicles. The dog went ballistic and howled in pain and rage as it rolled about the dusty floor trying to shake the cat off. The owner shouted and hollered at Tay to stop the fight. It wasn't a fair fight, and he didn't want the cat damaging his dog's chance at breeding. He had a bitch lined up for this one, and a litter of puppies could make him a few grand.

The dog finally managed to chomp its jaws down on the cat's tail and pulled with all its might and fury. It yanked and flung the cat against the wooden pallets. Blood sprayed across the dirty floor as it was thrown away.

Jesus-fucking-Christ, Darren thought as he saw the twin red gristly orbs of the dog's bollocks hanging between its back legs like a pair of clackers.

The dog fell onto its side, whining in pain as blood gushed from out of its shredded scrotum. Even then its merciless owner shouted for it to kill. Obedience still overrode the pain, and it forced itself to its feet just in time for the cat to spring once more at its exposed testicles.

The cat grabbed on like it was playing with a kitten's toy and sunk its claws and teeth into one of the firm round eggs and tore it from its connective tubes.

The dog cried out in pain and latched its jaws around the cat's neck and shook it from side to side, oblivious to the lightning strikes of the cat's claws about its eyes and muzzle.

After what seemed like minutes, the dog dropped the bloodied rag that had been the cat and fell to the floor panting and howling in pain. Even though the pool of blood that was expanding rapidly around its haunches would mean its death shortly, the dog had won. The cat lay, neck broken, throat completely obliterated, on its side, still.

Darren saw G laughing with Tay and accepting a wad of notes. The dog's owner had entered the ring and was swearing and jumping up and down on the cat's dead body as his prize money maker bled to death beside it.

When the aftermath of the fighting had died down and most of the people had left, Darren moved aside the pallets and squatted down to the dead cat. He felt sickened by what he had just witnessed, and the limp, cooling body in his hands made him doubt once more the cat's supernatural ability. Poor little bugger, he thought, as he shoved it into the rucksack and went to find G, hoping he would still keep up his end of the deal and dump the thing miles away, just to be on the safe side.

Back at the flats, G made a disgusted face and took the rucksack off of Darren. "Sure, I'll get it done, but you're going to owe me if you want it taking miles."

Darren sighed and reluctantly nodded his head.

G started to close the front door in Darren's face, muttering something about Darren having a few screws loose, but if he wanted to waste his money on some cat, then, whatever.

Darren felt apprehensive about whether G would keep to his word. He didn't dare ask for proof as that would insinuate that he thought G untrustworthy. Such a sign of disrespect would not go down well with the man.

As he walked across the car park towards his block, the foyer door swung open, and Cat-Man Stan came out carrying a plastic bag of dried cat food to distribute in the bowls he left by the skips for the local strays. It was good that he was up and about and carrying on as normal after the horrific ordeal the cat had put him through. Darren reassured himself that he had done the right thing in getting G to dispose of the body. The cat had been a vicious, dangerous animal; imagine what it could have done to a child or a baby? He was certain he had done the right thing. He had felt bad seeing the cat's dead body for himself, but he hoped the little bastard would stay dead this time.

Darren jogged up the slope towards the foyer door when he heard Cat-Man Stan call out for him. He tried to pretend not to hear, but the old man came running up to him and grabbed him by the arm. Darren turned and looked at the big-bearded, little, old man.

"You need to come with me, quick," Cat-Man said urgently and used his key fob to open the foyer door. Darren rolled his eyes heavenward and followed.

"So how many times has he come back?" Cat-Man said as they waited for the lift to stop.

Darren frowned with faked confusion.

Cat-Man was getting more agitated. "You know exactly what I'm on about. How many times has the cat come back since I got rid of it?"

"Once. This morning."

Cat-Man nodded and unlocked his front door. "So, do you now believe that this animal isn't ordinary?"

"There has to be a rational explanation," Darren started.

"Oh, there is an explanation, but it's far from rational." Cat-Man marched down the hallway of his flat and into the kitchen. Darren sat down at his dining table.

"Cats don't come back from the dead. Today, I saw him dead with my own eyes." Darren noticed a red leather-bound book on the table. It was called The Mythological Cat. A slip of paper stuck out flagging a bookmark.

Cat-Man switched the kettle on and leaned against the kitchen counter. "And where is the body now?"

"Err, I'm having a friend dispose of it," Darren said with a little shame.

Cat-Man gasped and put his hands to his face. "You must get it back now! Your friend will die!"

Darren laughed uneasily. "Don't you think that's a bit melodramatic?" But then he remembered the accident the previous day and the fatality of the RSPCA man.

Cat-Man sat down opposite him and peered gravely at the book on the table. His liver-spotted hand shook as he opened the book on the bookmarked page and turned it round to face Darren.

A black etched sketch of a sinister-looking cat with the words 'aeterna maledictio feline' above it seemed to be what Cat-Man wanted him to look at. There were a few references to a songwriter called Harry S. Miller dated at the end of the nineteenth century, along with photographs of some very old newspaper clippings detailing what appeared to be a series of unconnected accidents. A ship sinking, a train crash, children drowning, a death involving explosives, and even a hot air balloon catching fire.

Cat-Man stabbed a finger at the picture of the cat in the book and started to sing.

"Dar was ole Mister Johnson, he had troubles on his own,
He had an ole yaller cat that couldn't leave its home."

Cat-Man's voice was astounding. He sang what was obviously an old folk song. The accent and voice sounded exactly like an old, American negro.

Darren listened as the old man carried on his song. "He tried everything he knew to keep the cat away. Even sent it to de preacher, an' he tole it for to stay."

Cat-Man's hands beat on the table, one beat every other second.

"But de cat came back. He couldn't stay no longer. Yes, de cat came back de very next day.

"De cat came back -- thought she were a goner. But de cat came back, for it wouldn't stay away."

Cat-Man opened his eyes and stared straight into Darren's. "This song is about you."

Darren laughed uneasily and shook his head. "Just because the song mentions a Mister Johnson, doesn't mean it's me."

Cat-Man sighed deeply. "No, it doesn't. I didn't mean literally. The song is rumoured to be based on truth." He pointed at more song lyrics on the page. "This song is about a cat that keeps coming back, defying the laws of science." He stood dramatically, eyes wide, the chair toppling backwards. "Defying death itself!"

Darren opened his mouth to say something, but the old man shouted before he could utter a word.

"Aeterna maledictio feline!"

"Ate a what?"

"It means everlasting cat curse." Cat-Man sat back down and leafed through some pages of the book and stopped at a picture showing hieroglyphs of the Ancient Egyptians. A sketch depicting their worshipping of cats and how they saw them as sacred creatures filled the page. "There are legends of immortal cats dating back to these times. Every so often there are stories of cats that seemingly defy death. We've all heard the saying that they have nine lives. Well, where do you think it originates from?"

Darren tried not to laugh. "Look, I'm the first to admit this cat is a bit weird, that it is a plucky, if not lucky, little bastard. Come on, there has to be a rational explanation."

Cat-Man slammed his fists onto the table. "I tell you, I killed it."

"Okay, there are some things I can't explain, but, come on, an immortal fucking cat. Surely, if there was any truth in this, then some weird Omen-y type coincidental accident would have befallen you when you tried to kick its head in, or when I took it to the dogfight."

"You what?" Cat-Man recoiled in horror.

Darren looked down, ashamed. "I didn't know what my friend had planned. I just asked him to get rid of the bloody thing, take it miles away and dump it or something."

"What happened?"

"It, err, pretty much killed a prize-winning fighter dog before it had its throat ripped out."

Cat-Man went pale and closed his eyes. "Where is it now?"

"Like I said before," Darren said, pointing a thumb in the direction of the next block of flats, "my friend has it in the flats next door. He's going to dump it somewhere far away."

"Go and get it now before your friend is killed."

Darren stood up, still refusing to believe all this nonsense.

"If the cat is as you believe it to be, a normal, ordinary cat, and you are certain that it is dead, then what are you so afraid of?" Cat-Man asked Darren, even though he knew the answer.

Darren slumped back onto the chair. "If this is the case, what the fuck do I do about it?"

Cat-Man closed the book and pushed it towards him. "There is nothing you can do apart from the same thing the Ancient Egyptians did: worship it. Go save your friend before anyone else gets hurt. That is no ordinary cat. It is a god."

Darren thumped his fists upon the glossy black paint of G's front door even though he knew it was too late and the big man wasn't home. He slumped onto the beige carpet and put his face in his hands. He was so tired. It's all going to be okay, he tried telling himself. He'd take the cat in. Hell, he'd even call it fucking Tiddles if it meant no one else would get hurt.

How bad could it really be? He recalled the state of the hallway the morning after he took it in. But that's because this thing is a street cat, surely it can be trained.

Darren checked the time on his phone. It had been at least an hour since he dropped the cat off with G. If he hadn't been listening to Cat-Man talk endless piles of drivel that he was worryingly starting to believe, he may have been able to stop him from going. He hoped that whoever G had given the body to, to dispose of, just flung it out of a car window and kept driving.

The squeak of the lift moving up the shaft woke him up. He was surprised he had fallen asleep outside G's door. He was further surprised when he noticed it was dark outside.

The lift pinged, the door slid open, and G stepped out of the compartment. He was soaked. Had it been raining? When he saw Darren, his eyes went wide and his nostrils flared. Darren was no master at reading people's body language, but he knew G was extremely pissed off. Immediately he jumped to his feet and took on a cowering pose. The hall light showed that the big man was drenched in not just water but a fair amount of blood, too. His face was a crisscross network of bloody scratches. One or two strands of his dreadlocks had been plucked from his head, leaving gory patches that leaked down his forehead. He roared and slammed into Darren, grabbing two handfuls of his coat and pushed him up against the black front door. Darren yelped and doubled over as G drove a huge fist into his belly.

When G grabbed another handful of Darren's coat, Darren pulled away and shrugged the coat off. Realising he was free, he turned and ran through the door leading to the stairwell. Darren was a scrawny bastard and could move quickly if he had to, and he had to right now. He ran down the stairs as quickly as he could, the manic shouts of G from above assuring he kept going as quick as he could.

The big man didn't follow him. He didn't have to; he knew where he lived. Darren ran to his block of flats and only stopped when the doors of his own lift slid shut.

His phone bleeped. A text message from G. YOU HAD BETTER KEEP RUNNING AS I'M PUTTING A TARGET ON YOUR HEAD

Darren let out a solitary sob.

He knew what this meant.

G would have all his friends and followers in his crime syndicate hunting for him.

He'd probably put a bounty on him, some ridiculous money or drug-related incentive for his capture or death. The phone pinged again, a picture this time.

A man sat in a mangled heap behind a steering wheel. His face was so bloodied and torn apart it was unrecognisable. Lacerations covered every exposed piece of his dark skin. The window and door beside the driver of the car was smashed and mangled by a large, wet rock. The rock had bashed in and crumpled the side of the man's head and Darren could make out a meaty splatter strewn across its jagged edges. The man was obviously dead. The words beneath the photo told Darren everything he needed to know.

MY BROTHER.

Darren thanked whatever god was watching over him that he'd got a wallet full of money. Hopefully, that same deity would miraculously fill up the overdraft on his bank account he had just emptied.

Darren stood on the platform in the dark.

The station was deserted apart from him.

The neon clock clicked over to nine p.m., and, in the distance, two white pinpoints of light broke the claustrophobic blackness.

He half expected to see G and his posse come hurtling down the ramp to the platform, ready to end his life. The train screeched to a halt and the doors swished open. He got on.

A few seconds later the train pulled out of the station. The orange streetlights of the town around and above streaked past like roman candles.

He had come straight to the station after a quick stop at his flat. A purple plastic envelope held all his important papers and passport. He figured G or his friends would break into his place at some point. The last thing he wanted them to have was all his private details.

He thought about the cat. It always returned in the morning, but Darren knew he would be several hundred miles away by the time the sun came up.

When he had seen the multimedia message G had sent him with the photograph of his dead brother, he switched his phone off immediately. He dared not turn it back on.

Couldn't they trace you by your mobile phones?

He didn't know if G knew how to do that, but he sure as shit didn't want to find out.

He couldn't believe what he was doing, and he had no idea whether he would be welcome or not, but he didn't have any other choice. There were no other options available to him.

Over the four hours of the train journey, the blackness out of the window changed from multitudes of city lights to the unbroken pitch blackness of countryside.

Darren was going to see his father.

The train stopped at a remote station. Two platforms with small red-bricked buildings dotted about, disused for years. The station was empty. The one shop, a small café, which had seemingly been there forever, was naturally closed. The ancient analogue clock that swung on rusted chains told him the time was nearly one a.m. The station was exactly the same when he was a kid when he had last seen it. No modernisation had brought it into the twenty-first century.

The train station which time forgot.

Darren jogged up the platform, as the train left him truly alone. A small brick shelter sat above a set of stone stairs, their steps shiny and worn from years of use. He grabbed the old iron handrail and descended into the poorly lit underpass.

He couldn't believe there hadn't been any work done on the bloody thing in all this time. It was ridiculous. The underpass was lit with half a dozen bulbs in steel cages. Water dripped everywhere into a massive puddle that stretched across the uneven concrete.

Darren's footsteps echoed through the tunnel under the two railway lines. It was like something from a horror film, this underpass, wet filthy walls and flickering lights.

He hurried up the flight of steps leading out of the underpass and up the empty platform towards the exit.

A noise made him freeze.

A cat's meow.

Oh, fuck no, not here!

Darren spun around, looking for the graceful walk of his feline nemesis.

Nothing to see. He heard it again and snapped his head around to find its source. "Oh, Jesus fucking Christ." He breathed a sigh of relief when he saw it was just the station clock creaking on its rusty chains. His heart thudded in his chest but he still managed a solitary laugh.

He would have called for a taxi, but the phone box outside the station had been vandalised recently.

His shoes crunched on the smashed glass, and he gazed pitifully at the black handset with its explosion of wires.

Even if he did have the courage to turn his mobile phone on, he knew the chances of there being enough reception to even search the internet for a taxi company were slim to none. Reluctantly, he started the two-mile trek to his father's house.

Darren's folks had divorced and split up when he was a kid. He moved with his mother from one boyfriend to another. Each man she shacked up with lived further and further away from his father. Eventually, they became estranged. His father was always portrayed as the bad guy, the two-timing cheat who did the dirty on him and his mother when he was just eight years old. The truth of the matter was that his father couldn't stand his mother's descent into drugs and alcoholism after the seemingly endless postnatal depression, and he had sought love and compassion somewhere else. The first time his mother had shown interest in him was when they split up, and she took him with her despite his father's protests.

Darren, himself, had found out all about this as a teenager when he decided to contact his father. But, by then, he was a shitbag, just like his mother. Regular drug use and theft saw him in constant trouble with the law, so when his long-lost father offered to put him up for the weekend in his place in the country, he had agreed. After numerous phone calls, filling in various gaps that had been missed, Darren's father sent him the money to travel the four hours to stay with him for his eighteenth birthday. Darren had spent the money on speed, weed, and beer.

So, here he was, walking up roads he hadn't stepped on for nearly thirty years, heading towards a father that he really didn't remember much at all. The closer he got, the more embarrassed he felt. There was no way his father would have anything to do with him.

He cursed himself. What the hell was he thinking?

A sign at an entrance by the side of the road told him what he needed to know.

JOHNSON AND SON RIDING SCHOOL

He remembered his mum saying the woman his dad had cheated on her with had been a stuck-up bitch into horses, so it was no surprise to see they had started their own business. But... son?

Darren stopped and stared at the word SON. He had no right to be here. His father had obviously gotten on with his life, as any strong man would have.

Fuck it, Darren decided to himself. He would walk back to the train station and sleep rough on one of the benches. It wouldn't be the first time he's had a cold, wet night's sleep. He knew he had enough money to make it into London. He would get the first train away in the morning and decide what the hell to do from then on when he hit the big city.

A scuffling came from behind him, and a bright light shone in his face.

"My god, you're sodden," the man in the wax jacket said, lowering the torch. "You must come in and dry off for a bit."

Darren opened his mouth to protest, but the man waved his hand towards the entrance to the drive.

"Come on, don't worry about me. I'm certainly not worried about you," the man said, chuckling happily. "Not many psychopaths would be out in this weather, and I think if you were a potential burglar, you would at least have a vehicle of some sort. So, I deduce that you are either lost or here for another reason."

Darren was taken aback by the man's confident attitude and the Sherlock Holmes bullshit he was spouting. He followed the man, the torch shining a bright trajectory over the muddy driveway. By the sound of the man, he was younger than him, and he had the accent of someone who had been raised in this area but spent many years at a good university. There was little he could see of the man's features other than his dark knee-length wax jacket and his green wellington boots. They approached a large house, dark and ominous with just a solitary light on downstairs.

A security light came on outside the house as they neared, and Darren shot a glance at the man.

A youngish-looking face smiled out at him from beneath a flat cap. He looked regal like he could be an heir to the throne.

"I bet you wish we were still in the dark, don't you?" the man said and laughed heartily before clapping him on the shoulder. He was a dead ringer for Prince Harry. Darren shrugged and allowed himself to be led into the house.

The grey-haired lady who sat at a large, wooden, kitchen table looked startled when the man brought Darren in. She quickly made sure that the purple dressing gown she wore was fastened appropriately and stood up smiling. "Edward, who is your friend? He looks drenched, poor thing."

Edward whipped off his flat cap and ran a hand through thick brown hair and slammed something down on the table. A brace of dead pheasants. He cracked the shotgun that he had been carrying and removed the unused cartridges before placing them on the table.

He caught Darren's startled expression at the gun and dead birds and laughed. "I found him passing by the front. He's not much of a talker yet."

The woman didn't seem to be that much concerned to have a complete stranger in her home.

She turned towards Darren and smiled warmly. "Come in and sit down, my dear. I'll put the kettle on. You look like you could do with a warm drink." She gestured towards a chair at the table, and Darren automatically sat down in it, gazing about him.

The kitchen was a traditional country manor kitchen. Large, expensive-looking, antique wooden furniture displayed crockery that was probably worth more money than he would see in a year. A huge, black stove dominated the wall in front of him. The only other thing on that wall was a large crucifix.

"Edward, dear, go and find this man some dry clothes and a towel, for Heaven's sake," the woman said sternly to the man who had just that moment sat down at the table. He rolled his eyes and winked at Darren conspiratorially. "Okay, mother."

After the man called Edward had left the kitchen, the woman turned to Darren. "You look flabbergasted. I'm sorry if my son has startled you somewhat."

Darren shook his head and smiled, finally finding words in his mouth. "I… umm… I've come from the station. I think I got lost."

The woman nodded as though it were a regular occurrence. "Where were you headed for?"

Shit, Darren thought and hesitated.

His hesitancy didn't go unnoticed by the lady either. "You don't have a place to stay, do you?"

Darren sheepishly stared at the table and grumbled a barely audible, "no."

The woman smiled sympathetically and placed a mug of tea before him. As she moved to get milk and sugar, she spoke. "You must stay here tonight. You can't go back out there in this weather. Get some dry clothes on you, and we'll find out what to do in the morning. Stephen, my husband, will have all the answers, I'm sure."

Well, that was the confirmation that Darren needed. Stephen Johnson was the name of his father. "Err, is your husband about still at this hour?"

"Oh, no, he's an early riser. He sees to the horses. I don't know if you noticed the sign, but we're a riding school." The woman's face lit up with obvious pride in their business.

Darren breathed a sigh of relief and sipped at the tea. "Thank you for your generosity."

"Why, any other good Christian person would do the same." She beamed at him and flicked her eyes to the crucifix on the wall.

When the man called Edward, her son, returned, the woman, whose name was Harriet, instructed him to show their visitor to the guest room, where he could make himself comfortable and use the en-suite bathroom.

Darren wallowed in the hot bath water. It was definitely the home of his father. His mother, the deluded old hag, had nicknamed Harriet--Harriet the chariot, due to her love of horses. She had told lewd lies about rumours of inter-species sex and how she probably got off riding her beloved horses.

His mother was a bad woman.
He knew that from a young age.

The woman downstairs seemed wonderful, like the mother he should have had. He had fucked his life up so much.

That should have been him downstairs with Harriet. She should have been his Stepmother. Well, she kind of was, but Darren knew he wasn't part of this family. He didn't belong here. He had given up his last chance at that as a wayward teenager. He wondered how old Edward was.

"Shit," Darren cursed his eighteen-year-old self. That weekend away his father had offered him all those years ago could have saved his fucking life. He could have rekindled things, started afresh, had a little brother, gone to college or something.

He thought about all he had achieved in the eighteen years since and felt like letting the luxurious warm bath water close over his head forever.

Darren made his mind up that he would sneak out of the house at first light. The last thing he wanted to do was bring unnecessary strife on this family.

The

Very

Next

Day...

The disorientation of waking up in a place not just unknown to him in daylight, but altogether alien, startled Darren at first. Then he remembered the events of the previous night. Holy shit, I'm at my father's.

He sat up in the guest bed of this unknown house in the country. The dim light of dawn cast a blue hue over the room. A chair at the foot of the bed displayed his washed, dried, and folded clothes. His wallet, phone, and keys sat on top of the pile.

He quickly pulled his clothes on and opened the door as quietly as he could. The interior of the house was darkened. Thick curtains were drawn across the windows. He spotted the staircase and stepped down them. Surprisingly, none of them creaked with the stereotype of this kind of situation.

Darren reached what he presumed was the front door and, after unfastening numerous bolts, locks, and chains, let himself out into the cool morning.

"You look more like your mother now than ever," a gruff voice came from his left as he shut the door.

Darren froze. It must be his father.

Darren turned slowly towards the owner of the voice.

A tall man leant against the front of the house, a mug in one hand and a cherry-red pipe in the other. He had a full head of grey hair, his face long and haggard.

"How did you know it was me?" Darren asked, feeling beyond awkward.

His father glanced at him from the corner of his eyes and puffed out a grey cloud of smoke. "I had my suspicions when Harriet told me we had an unexpected visitor. I checked your wallet."

"Fair enough," Darren mumbled. After all this time he was lost for words, even though this man was his biological father he may as well be a total stranger.

Stephen Johnson knocked back the dregs of his morning beverage and sat the mug on the windowsill behind him. "So, what do you want, Darren?"

Darren opened his mouth to tell his dad that he didn't want anything when a horrific whinnying broke his concentration.

His father went wide-eyed and started jogging towards a row of red stables. Darren followed.

He saw his father stop at one of the stalls and raise his arms in the air. The wooden door which covered the stall bucked and shook as something heavy hit it hard.

"Whoa, whoa," his dad shouted into the stable, his arms flapping up and down slowly.

The horse struck out at the wooden door again, and they both heard the sound of wood splintering.

"Get back," his father screamed at him, shooing him away with his hands.

The horse kicked out once more, and the stall door crashed open, narrowly missing Stephen.

A large, chestnut horse bolted out of the stable, its coat slick with sweat.

It pranced around in some weird dance on its hind legs, the front ones kicking madly at the air.

Darren's knowledge of horses extended little further than that of a normal uninterested person, but he knew that they were strong, and he knew that if one of those flailing hooves connected with him it would hurt seriously.

He staggered back as the horse veered towards him, looking at his father for guidance.

Stephen raised his hands and backed away to a wood-beamed fence behind him. Not taking an eye off the bucking creature, he flicked up the latch on a wide gate and swung it wide open.

The horse reared and kicked and puffed out breath from its flared nostrils.

Stephen approached the horse with his arms raised, shouting, narrowly avoiding the paddling hooves. "We need to get him in the paddock. Let him run it off."

Darren's heart pummeled fiercely in his chest. All he could think of was those lethal hooves. His father, Stephen, swerved out of the way as the horse danced closer to him.

Darren knew he needed to do something. Whatever was up with the horse could cause it to hurt someone or itself. He raised his arms and started shouting in a perfect imitation of his father.

The horse's hooves crashed down hard, splattering them both with mud. They continued their open-armed gestures until their strange choreography drove the horse sideways, towards the entrance of the enclosed paddock.

The chestnut stallion galloped across the enclosure, kicking up clouds of dust. Stephen slammed the gate shut and leaned against it to catch his breath. He bent double and spat out a wad of dusty brown phlegm.

"Whoa, I think you'd better call a vet or something," Darren said, gazing across the riding ground.

Stephen peered ahead to see what had happened.

The horse laid on its side on the dirt, its legs twitching.

"For God's sake," Stephen muttered, straightening up and pressing his fist into the small of his back. "I think it's having a heart attack. I'm going to the house to ring the vet and get my gun."

Darren was appalled at the latter part of his father's comment.

A gun.

He had seen enough animal brutality in the past twenty-four hours to last him a lifetime.

This was his cue to leave.

He waited until he saw his father vanish into the house before turning away.

Darren jogged around the circular paddock, deliberately avoiding setting eyes on the horse.

He could hear its legs smacking against the ground, troubled grunts coming from its nose as it fought whatever was happening to it.

As he passed, it caught his eye.

It lay on the ground near the entrance to the farm, its rubbery lips drew back, speckled with thick white foam, muscles straining as it tried to right itself.

The horse's abdomen bulged unnaturally, and something beneath the dark hair and skin moved.

Darren stood and stared in sickened fascination.

Something pressed itself against the horse's abdominal wall from within. The lump, which moved like a shape beneath a brown silk blanket, was triangular and not much bigger than a baseball. Four new protrusions rose near the surface of the horse's skin.

A spot of terror formed in the pit of Darren's stomach like an ink spot. Subconsciously he heard his father shouting as he raced across the field, but all he could focus on was the sight before him.

The sound of the thrashing agonized horse drowned out everything.

Realisation had already added body to the terror in his belly, and it exploded like a mushroom cloud inside his chest.

Needle sharp barbs pricked through the horse's skin and scoured red weeping lines. Sharp incisors bit a hole at the centre of the triangular protrusion.

The cat.

Darren watched, transfixed, totally oblivious to the tears that ran freely down his face. The cat slowly and methodically chewed, raked, and dug its way out of the horse's stomach. It pushed its gore-matted head through the orifice it had made. The blood lubricated its perverted rebirth.

Darren's legs had given out at some point during this, and he sat, forehead resting against the fence, sobbing in terror.

The first time he paid attention to his father was when he heard him groan and curse at the situation before them.

The cat forced itself through the ragged hole and plopped onto the soil, its grey fur slickened by the visceral juices.

Darren looked up at his father and through a mouth clogged with snot, spit, and dust cried, "I'm so sorry."

His father nodded. He couldn't begin to understand what was going on, but the expression on Darren's face told him he was guilty of something. He pulled out a thick envelope from inside his coat and flung it on the ground between Darren's thighs. "I don't know what trouble you're in, and I don't want to. Go and never come back."

Darren picked up the envelope, absent-mindedly nodding, eyes never leaving the cat.

He got to his feet and backed away from his father, the cat, and the dying horse and watched as the cat casually washed the blood off its fur. His father raised his gun and the cat couldn't give a shit, just carried on licking its gory paw and rubbing it behind one of its bloody ears. He thought he could hear it purring. It shot its yellow eyes in his direction and meowed.

Darren turned as the gun went off once.

As he stumbled up the driveway, the agonizing whinnies of the dying horse were silenced by the second shot.

The early morning sunlight transformed dew drops on grass blades to dripping diamonds. The woods were alive with birdsong after a heavy night's roosting and sheltering from the torrential downpour. The beauty of the day was completely lost upon the figure shuffling in the zombie-like stagger of those suffering extreme shock or exhaustion.

Darren's feet scuffed along the muddy track beside the winding road, only the slightly raised grass verge bashing against his ankle stopped him from walking into the narrow ditch that ran beside. He still clutched the envelope his father had forced into his hand. His knuckles strained white as he clung onto it.

His face was slack, jaw hanging as his mind tried to process events that were beyond anyone's comprehension. His stomach was a burning acidic knot of apprehension. The two gunshots still reverberated inside his head, one for the horse, one for the cat.

The sheer lack of emotion his father had shown at such an unnatural situation was equally as startling.

He hadn't planned his journey, had just let his feet guide him wherever they wanted, just as long as it was away. He momentarily surfaced from amidst the thick fog of his thoughts to notice he was once again at the train station.

The platform was full of suited commuters armed with laptop cases and metallic thermos mugs. They were dressed in stereotypical morbid colours, like attendees to a funeral, albeit one with Wi-Fi access.

The pointed yellow face of the train approaching appeared in the distance, and the crowd moved as one closer to the platform edge. Darren shuffled onto the train and sat in the nearest seat.

The train pulled away. He studied the envelope, just a normal blank document envelope containing something an inch thick. He suspected money. Money to pay him off, to make sure he wouldn't return, no doubt. His father had obviously not told his new family that this was his long-lost son. That was evident, but he thought they would figure it out.

When he opened the envelope, he wasn't surprised to find his suspicions confirmed. A wad of purple twenties was banded together with a thick red rubber band. It was at least a couple of thousand pounds. Along with the money was a slip of yellow paper and a solitary Polaroid photograph.

He pulled the photo out. A thirty-odd year younger version of his father stood leaning against a typically garish eighties wallpaper of oranges, golds, and browns. In his arms was a cute, dimple-cheeked little boy, eyes practically twinkling with love and adoration for this man. The man gazed with similar warmth and humour.

A happy father and son.

Just to the bottom of the photograph, a photobomb, a smearing stain on an otherwise wonderful glimpse into his past, a Smirnoff vodka bottle, half empty on a coffee table. A constant reminder of his mother tainting the image.

He flipped it over, and in handwriting that had almost faded into nothing was the date and the words me and my boy.

Tears ran freely down Darren's face as he read the few sentences on the slip of paper.

`Darren,

I figure this was what you were after. Have the money, but take this, too, my only memento from a life long forgotten.

Your Father'

He carefully folded the note and put the contents back in the envelope. A suit opposite him peered curiously at the wad of cash from the corner of his eyes. An expression of contempt dragged the corners of his mouth down.

Darren suspected he thought the usual, rough looking scrawny man with a wad of cash, must be drug money or something else illegal. He scowled at the man and thrust the envelope inside his coat pocket.

He wished it was drug money. That wouldn't come with such guilt and emotional torture. Part of him wanted to return it to his father, but he knew he was at a dead end. If he went back to his place, or even the town or surrounding suburbs, G would track him down and kill him.

Luckily, being someone with a checkered past, Darren knew people who may be able to help him out of his shitty situation.

For a price, he knew someone who could set him up with all the documents necessary to create a fake identity.

As the express train hurtled into the country's capital, Darren had formulated a plan of action.

"And do you have any luggage to declare, Sir?" the pristinely attired man asked as he scrutinized Darren's passport, searching for something untoward. Not many solitary dishevelled men carrying a bunch of banknotes and no bags bought tickets for the soonest flight available from the country. It just didn't happen in real life. It was something from the movies.

Darren shook his head and stared about himself waiting for a couple of burly security guards to appear and whisk him away for a few questions. The airport clerk was stalling him. He knew it, repeatedly checking his passport, tapping the keys, smiling nervously.

Darren rubbed a hand over his five-day stubble, forced an awkward smile on his face, and leant conspiratorially over the counter. "You don't recognise me, do you?"

The young man visibly flinched at Darren's invasion of his personal space. He shook his head. "Should I?"

Darren straightened up, pushed his hand against his churning guts and laughed. "Hell, maybe you're too young kid. I'm Daz Johnson, lead singer of the band," he flicked his eyes about for inspiration, "The, err, Terminals."

The young man laughed with mild embarrassment. "I'm sorry, sir, I've not heard of your band."

Darren shrugged sheepishly. "It's no bother, man. Like I say, you're probably too young. We never really got that big anyway. There were tons of bands like ours in the early nineties." Darren surprised himself at the level of his improv bullshit. "We opened for Oasis once. I wrote Wonderwall!" He mentally cursed himself for the sheer audacity of that particular lie, but the airport clerk looked just as clueless as before.

His stomach churned once more. "Look, kid, can you give me my ticket or not, cuz I'm busting for the bog, and I think I'm going to go off like a chocolate fucking rocket in a minute."

The man clicked a button and handed him back his passport. An electronic whirr buzzed beside him and the clerk handed him a glossy plane ticket. "Here, sir, enjoy your flight to Kiev."

Darren rested his head against the departure lounge wall and stared at nothing. The crampy stomach knot of nerves he had felt since leaving his father's had changed into a queasy feeling. He prayed he wasn't coming down with a stomach bug or virus. The last thing he wanted was to be ill in some foreign country.

He didn't even know where Kiev was. He had eaten chicken kievs before, though, and they weren't that foreign, just chicken, garlic, and breadcrumbs.

There were a few people in the departure lounge, a middle-aged couple, robust and hard looking faces that looked incapable of humour. They sat, chatting away in German or whatever language it was, never giving one another eye contact or showing emotion.

Darren sat opposite a tall, scrawny, bald man in a suit. More devices than he had hands were nesting on and around him as he tapped at this, scrolled that, and spoke into this.

He wondered how he could concentrate on so many things at once.

Darren's stomach flipped, and he felt bile rise in his throat and subside again. He groaned and leaned his elbows on his knees.

A young couple with a toddler boy and girl showed a little concern and moved several seats further away, as though these valuable few inches would make the difference between contracting what could potentially be the bubonic plague or not.

Darren retched and saw them visibly flinch. He rushed to his feet and moved across the tiled flooring towards the toilets. He hoped he'd make it in time.

One hand clamped over his mouth, Darren palmed open the door and bounded into the toilets. He bent over the nearest sink and gagged so hard it made his eyes water and see stars. His mouth filled with corrosive bile, which he spat into the sink. A secondary wave of nausea rose, and this time, a flood of brown liquid splashed into the sink and dripped from his nose.

Darren caught his own wide-eyed reflection as something blocked his oesophagus. His eyes streamed as he choked and tried to dislodge the obstruction.

A man came out of the toilet and immediately saw Darren's predicament. "Oh, my God, are you choking?"

Darren nodded quickly. Mouth open, reddening face, it was obvious.

He thumped Darren on the back as hard as he could, but nothing happened. The man moved behind him and attempted to do something he'd only ever seen done on TV shows, the Heimlich manoeuvre. He brought his hands together beneath Darren's ribcage and squeezed hard.

Nothing happened the first time, other than Darren thinking this big bear of a man was going to snap a rib. The second time he felt the lump clogging up his throat shift a little. He motioned excitedly to the man that it was working.

The man repeated the procedure with increased vigour. It had an immediate effect. A lump shot out of Darren's mouth like a miniature comet with a pink puke tail trailing behind it.

Darren sucked in air and clung to the sink panting.

"What the fuck is that man?" the man asked, as he peered at the lump in the sink. It resembled a short, thick grey sausage. "Looks like something my cat brought up."

Darren gasped at his words. That's exactly what the mysterious lump looked like.

A furball.

The nondescript man patted Darren on the shoulder and left him to stare in disgust at the thing in the sink. Images of the cat forcing its way out of the horse's stomach replayed in glorious technicolour.

Could the demonic feline be growing inside of him now like a tumour?

Further images, this time not a recollection but an imagining of a small grey cat fetus swelling in the bowl of his stomach, marinating in the digestive juices.

Now he had brought this sausage-shaped clump of matted grey fur up, the ill feeling in his stomach had passed, but it was replaced with more panic.

What if the cat was growing inside of him?

Darren splashed water over his face and yanked out a strip of paper towels to dry himself.

All he knew was that he was getting on that plane in an hour's time.

Darren paid the counter girl for the small brown bottle of liquid laxative and put it in the bag he had brought from the liquor store.

He had absolutely no idea what the hell he was doing or whether it would work, but, as he headed towards the boarding gate, he unscrewed the cap from the laxatives and downed half the bottle. It was thick and foul tasting.

He didn't know how soon the stuff would take to kick in, but, as he jogged down the white inclining tunnel towards the plane to Kiev, he thought he felt his stomach bubble.

A dark-haired stewardess showed him to his seat, and he made a point of telling her he felt ill, and he wasn't sure if it was nerves or something he ate. He assured her he was okay for the flight. She made him aware of the sick bags and toilet before rushing off to aid another passenger.

The preflight procedures all went swimmingly, the stewards running through their safety choreography. Before he knew it, the plane was speeding down the tarmac.

The middle-aged couple he had noticed in the departure lounge sat beside him. Both had their eyes squeezed shut and their fingers interlocking. He wondered which of them was scared of flying.

Darren had never flown before, and his virgin voyage was certainly going to be one to remember.

The actual take-off he found quite exhilarating, the speed forcing him back into his seat and the smooth, yet terrifying, lurch as the wheels lifted from the terra-firma.

He felt the first worrisome squirm in his belly just as a light pinged on above his head, telling him he could unfasten his seatbelt. Good timing.

He felt as though a long slippery eel was sliding around his insides, and, when he felt its hot face push against his sphincter muscles, he ran to the toilet.

The cubicle was minute. He couldn't understand how people were rumoured to get off on getting off on aeroplanes. He was not a big man, but the space was very limited. He managed to just sit his buttocks on the cold, plastic, horseshoe toilet seat before what felt like a scalding hot octopus erupted from his arse, causing him to whimper.

He shat until his ring burned as brightly as that one in those Peter Jackson films.

Darren stopped on the toilet, hunched over, whilst his stomach bubbled and pulsated.

It was at least an hour and a half before he had the confidence to even attempt moving away from the besplattered throne.

When he thought he could shit no more, he pulled a half litre bottle of whisky from the bag from the liquor store and drank a large measure. It burned its way down his throat and ignited a fire in his empty belly.

Another stomach cramp made him scrunch up and hug his legs whilst his arsehole made a noise, not unlike whale song.

Then the lights went out.

Darren didn't panic. He had never flown before. This could be common during flights.

A faulty lightbulb perhaps?

Then the screams of a hundred or so people as the floor seemed to fall away from him.

The sheer speed in which the plane dropped caused Darren and the contents of the lavatory to fly upwards and smash headfirst against the cubicle ceiling. In the two seconds of disorientated waking darkness, Darren felt and smelt something hot and meaty splatter his face before the head injury caused loss of consciousness.

The Very Next Day...

Blackness.

Heat.

Burning pain.

Consciousness surged back, like a tidal wave of black pain.

The black was speckled with freckles of light, and it took Darren several minutes after his eyes stopped rolling around to figure out what they were.

Stars.

There shouldn't be stars.

But there shouldn't be pain, white-hot pain. Pain so excruciating it flicked his consciousness on and off like a dimmer switch on a light.

His head flopped on its side as he passed out again for a few seconds. When his eyes fluttered open he saw the wreckage. Chunks of metal, debris made of both man and manmade materials littered the surrounding area.

Everything was on fire.

Moans of other survivors broke through the clear night sky, like a perverse parody of the dawn chorus.

He couldn't see anyone else in detail, just the odd raised beckoning arm, black and skeletal. There was no sign of help yet.

Darren tried to move despite the pain.

Everything hurt, and he found he could only move his left arm and turn his head.

That was something. The rest of his body was constant agony.

He pushed the elbow of his working arm into the mud and forced himself up a few inches. When he saw the mangled ruined mess of his legs he almost fainted again.

A considerable amount of light showed the ruination of his lower half in sickening detail. His legs were completely destroyed, crushed into a mash of bones, blood and muscle.

The source of the light was a huge burning triangle of metal that jutted out of the ground like some kind of monolithic pyramid. Fire flickered and dripped all over it.

Darren slumped back into the mud, exhausted and beaten.

He was rewarded with another respite from the agony, as the exertion caused him to pass out again.

Sirens, not familiar sounding. Foreign.

Darren heard them far away, but even weird sounding sirens were better than none. A sign of rescuers on the way. He rolled his head in their direction, trying to concentrate beyond the field of devastation.

Something shifted in the wreckage in his line of vision. Something shrivelled, black, and charred.

Like a molten piece of plastic, this thing flipped and flopped on the mud like a salmon out of water.

Gradually, tiny embers of fire prickled it, and smoke whispered up as it changed in size.

The charred darkness began to lighten into a lobster red.

Bubbling yellow fat and pus trickled up from the ground and fattened great blisters upon the thing's skin.

A whoosh of fire engulfed the thing, and singed black fur began to transform into grey fur.

Two barely audible pops as eyeballs burst into existence inside its triangular head. Whiskers pricked back from its face, and the screeching cat's tongue sizzled back to normal inside its shrieking mouth.

The fire self-extinguished and the cat's frightened howls lowered into a deep snarl of fear and anger. The fur that spiked along its spine settled, and it stretched out its limbs to check their mobility.

The cat's yellow eyes, pupils large and dark, moved nonchalantly towards Darren.

Meow.

Darren could feel the threads of his sanity unravel at an alarming rate, as he could only watch as the regenerated cat moved stealthily closer. He was helpless.

It inched closer towards the one who took it in cautiously. It knew the man was incapacitated but remembered how threatening he could potentially be. *Meow*, it said again, testing the man's reaction to its presence. It just wanted to be loved, *safe*.

Why did his owners always turn so cruel?

Meow?

The man lay still, still was a good thing, no signs of aggression or threat. It crawled over to the man, his man, but remained alert to any signs of danger. The man's fingers reached out across the muddy grass.

Meow, it said one more time, and rubbed its mouth and nose against the man's fingers, in a gesture of affection. The man was hurt. He was covered in the wet stuff that leaked out of them, the kind that smelt and tasted nice.

It licked one of the man's fingertips and, sensing no danger, moved towards the man's chest.

Darren saw the twinkles of emergency vehicle lights in the distance. Using his last resources of energy, he grabbed the cat by its shaggy grey scruff and brought it up to his mouth. Ignoring the thrashing razor sharp claws that raked at his face, Darren opened his mouth and bit down hard.

Fur, skin, muscle and blood filled his mouth as he tore the cat away and roared through a mouthful of its throat. Darren spat the lump of gore from his mouth and hurled the tormenting impossible creature as hard as he could.

The cat's limp, rag doll body slapped into the burning jagged triangle of metal with a metallic clang. The tip of the plane's wing, which the cat hit, had been burning for ages. The fuel that had washed over it on impact saw to that. Even though it was partially embedded in the earth, it had been gradually leaning over. The collision with the hastily dying corpse of a flying feline was enough to speed up its descent.

The last thing Darren saw was a massive fiery triangle falling towards him before he was crushed and burned instantaneously with the coppery taste of cat blood on his tongue.

The

Very

Last

Day...

Brygida chopped the last of the sausage into small squares. There was always too much for her since her husband died, but, still, her children always brought her food.

We need to make sure you are eating enough, Mother. They would say.

She was old, though, not so much of an appetite these days, not for anything. There was little that Brygida enjoyed in her twilight years. Rheumatism wracked her joints all over. She carried too much weight, and, together, it made it hard for her to be as mobile as she once was. Her independence was important to her, though, and she was determined that she would die in her house.

I was born here, I shall die here! She had told her children when they had wanted her to live with them when their father died. They had complained and protested, but she was still their mother. She became immune to their whines and demands when they were still clutching at her apron strings.

A lot of their cousins had moved further into Europe, even to England and America, but she would never leave Poland. It was her home.

Brygida took the plate of chopped sausage, pushed open the solid door of the farmhouse and stood unsteadily on the wooden porch.

"Pochodzą moje koteczkami!" she shouted and made noise by vibrating the tip of her tongue against her few remaining front teeth. It sounded like a box of matches being shaken, dried rice in a pot. "Come, my kitty cats."

Across the fields, an overgrown adventure land, filled with no end of vermin and places to explore, came a series of catcalls as her cats wove their way through the tall grass. They darted from the dew-damp foliage and raced up to the porch steps.

There were six, all females of varying ages, mostly strays or pets who had chosen to bless her with their presence.

A seventh, a big, shabby tomcat, slunk behind them and up to Brygida's cats. She clucked her tongue and scowled in mock disgust.

"Oh, I now see why you weren't already clawing at my door," she said to the females who stared up at the plate imploringly. She addressed the new addition to the family, the grey cat. "Welcome, Mr, Szary," which was Polish for grey. "You come now, make me some beautiful kittens."

Brygida threw a lump of sausage to the grey tom, who slashed a paw at it and dug his claws into the cold fatty meat.

Brygida smiled as she watched him eat. His purring nearly drowned out the female cat's pines for food.

Brygida threw the remainder of the food to the cats and kept them in check if they tried to take more than what was theirs. The tom trotted up the steps and wound its way around her ankles, rubbing its furry body against her lovingly.

Even though it pained her, Brygida bent down and stroked him under the chin. "Mr Szary, you are a perfect gentleman, aren't you?"

Meow, the cat answered.

Her fingers came away red, " Mr Szary, you need a bath, stinky cat. But you are so handsome. You make me some lovely kittens. You have six wives now."

Mr Szary, the cat, twitched his whiskers and closed his eyes in bliss as his new owner scratched an itch behind his ear. Opening one eye, he surveyed his new home and built-in harem and simply said *Meow*!

Matthew Cash

Author Biography

Matthew Cash, or Matty-Bob Cash as he is known to most, was born and raised in Suffolk; which is the setting for his debut novel Pinprick. He is compiler and editor of Death by Chocolate, a chocoholic horror anthology, and the 12Days Anthology, head of Burdizzo Books and Burdizzo Bards and has numerous releases on Kindle and several collections in paperback.

He has always written stories since he first learnt to write and most, although not all tend to slip into the many-layered murky depths of the Horror genre.

His influences ranged from when he first started reading to Present day are, to name but a small select few; Roald Dahl, James Herbert, Clive Barker, Stephen King, Stephen Laws, and more recently he enjoys Adam Nevill, F.R Tallis, Michael Bray, Gary Fry, William Meikle and Iain Rob Wright (who featured Matty-Bob in his famous A-Z of Horror title M is For Matty-Bob, plus Matthew wrote his own version of events which was included as a bonus). He is a father of two, a husband of one and a zookeeper of numerous fur babies.

You can find him here:
www.facebook.com/pinprickbymatthewcash

https://www.amazon.co.uk/-/e/B010MQTWKK

PINPRICK

All villages have their secrets Brantham is no different. Twenty years ago after foolish risk-taking turned into tragedy Shane left the rural community under a cloud of suspicion and rumour. Events from that night remained unexplained, memories erased, questions unanswered. Now a notorious politician, he returns to his birthplace when the offer from a property developer is too good to decline. With big plans to haul Brantham into the 21st century, the developers have already made a devastating impact on the once quaint village. But then the headaches begin, followed by the nightmarish visions. Soon Shane wishes he had never returned as Brantham reveals its ugly secret.

VIRGIN AND THE HUNTER

Hi, I'm God. And I have a confession to make.

I live with my two best friends and the girl of my dreams, Persephone.

When the opportunity knocks, we are usually down the pub having a few drinks, or we'll hang out in Christchurch Park until it gets dark then go home to do college stuff. Even though I struggle a bit financially life is good, carefree.

Well, they were.

Things have started going downhill recently, from the moment I started killing people.

KRACKERJACK

Five people wake up in a warehouse, bound to chairs.

Before each of them, tacked to the wall are their witness testimonies.

They each played a part in labelling one of Britain's most loved family entertainers a paedophile and sex offender.

Clearly, revenge is the reason they have been brought here, but the man they accused is supposed to be dead.

Opportunity knocks and Diddy Dave Diamond has one last game show to host and it's a knockout.

KRACKERJACK2

Ever wondered what would happen if a celebrity faked their own death and decided they had changed their minds?

Two years ago, publicly shunned comedian Diddy Dave Diamond convinced the nation that he was dead only to return from beyond the grave to seek retribution on those who ruined his career and tainted his legacy.

Innocent or not only one person survived Diddy Dave Diamond's last ever game show, but the forfeit prize was imprisonment for similar alleged crimes.

Prison is not kind to inmates with those type of convictions and as the sole survivor finds out, but there's a sudden glimmer of hope.

Someone has surfaced in the public eye claiming to be the dead comedian

FUR

The old aged pensioners of Boxford are very set in their ways, loyal to each other and their daily routines. With families and loved ones either moved on to pastures new or maybe even the next life, these folk can get dependent on one another.

But what happens when the natural ailments of old age begin to take their toll?

What if they were given the opportunity to heal and overcome the things that make everyday life less tolerable?

What if they were given this ability without their consent?

When a group of local thugs attack the village's wealthy Victor Krauss, they unwittingly create a maelstrom of events that not only could destroy their home but everyone in and around it.

Are the old folk the cause or the cure of the horrors?

Other Releases by Matthew Cash

Novels

Virgin and the Hunter

Pinprick

Novellas

Ankle Biters

KrackerJack

KrackerJack 2

Clinton Reed's Fat

Illness

Hell and Sebastian

Waiting for Godfrey

Deadbeard

The Cat Came Back

Frosty [coming 2019]

Short Stories

Why Can't I Be You?

Slugs and Snails and Puppydog Tails

Oldtimers

Hunt the C*nt

Anthologies Compiled and Edited by Matthew Cash of Burdizzo Books

Death by Chocolate

12 Days STOCKING FILLERS

12 Days: 2016

12 Days: 2017

The Reverend Burdizzo's Hymnbook*

SPARKS*

*with Em Dehaney

Under the Weather [with Em Dehaney & Back Road Books]

Anthologies Featuring Matthew Cash

Rejected for Content 3: Vicious Vengeance

JEApers Creepers

Full Moon Slaughter

Full Moon Slaughter 2

Down the Rabbit Hole: Tales of Insanity

Visions from The Void [edited by Jonathan Butcher & Em Dehaney]

Collections

The Cash Compendium Volume One

The Cash Compendium Continuity [coming 2019]

Website:
www.Facebook.com/pinprickbymatthewcash

Copyright © Matthew Cash 2019